The Four Keys

The Beginning

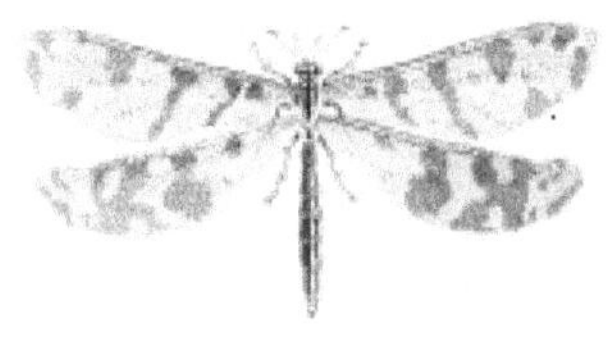

J.C. Lucas

Copywrite

Dedication

To my wonderful husband. Thank you for your endless support and encouragement. And thank you for getting groceries or dinner so that I could finish writing.

Hopefully one day my stories will be on Audible so that you can "read" them.

I love you more.

Chapter One

Becca

S*omething* was coming. My blood sizzled as I ran through the woods. Fairies on either side of me giggled as they chased each other, and the air grew thick and muggy. Raising my gaze to the blue sky, I searched for storm clouds, but there were none.

My skin pimpled with goosebumps as an ominous feeling coursed through me.

"Eira!" I shouted to the blond fairy gliding on the wind in front of me. "Something isn't right." I raced ahead to where she stopped mid-air, the others quieted beside us.

"Every bone in my body is telling me that we need to find the rest of the family and warn them"

Eira and I had been friends forever and I couldn't remember a day without her by my side. Mother said that Eira took to me from the moment I was born, pledging to keep me safe as long as she was able.

Blue eyes flashed as she searched for danger in the thick woods.

I didn't have to worry that she wouldn't take me seriously, she always had, why, I don't know. She had an innate belief in everything I told her, much which always came true.

Father said it was the "sight" and that I was touched by the gods. That it skipped a generation, and they were fortunate to have a daughter such as I.

Right now, I didn't feel special. I felt lost and alone, and I wanted to call out for my parents. But I knew that if I did, it would only bring destruction down upon me.

Motioning to the other fairies, Eira gave them instructions and they scattered just as a thunderous noise rocked the forest... and then the screaming began.

∞

Rumbling came from every direction. Turning in circles, I tried to decide the best direction to travel. Eira did the same before landing beside my ear.

"Do exactly as I say Becca, don't deviate. It's a matter of life and death, and we must keep you from harm," she whispered quietly. "Now... run to the berry patch we visited the other day. Whatever you see or hear, do *not* let it stop you. We have to get there, and soon. If I should leave you, do not stop. Not for anything! Go to the patch and hide in the brambles."

Breathing deeply, I ran.

Off the path and through the green woods, dragonflies and pixies scattered into the air as my feet pounded around them.

Frightening creatures tore through the village, bodies of our clan lay twisted and mangled on the ground around their homes. My heart thumped faster with each step I took, but I didn't worry about the noise from my flight, as the screams grew louder drowning everything out.

The rise and fall of the horrible sounds were in tune with the pounding of my heart. I wanted nothing more than to run to them and help. Even so, I knew that I had to do exactly as Eira said or else I would end up just another dead body strewn across the forest floor.

I had no idea who or what these creatures were, but I heard them shouting to *look for the gray eyed ones. To kill them all.* Unfortunately for me, I had gray eyes, and I stood no chance against them.

Not much further, and you'll be at the berry patch.

Not much further, and you'll be at the berry patch.

I repeated that mantra over and over in my head as sweat trickled down my back and Eira sat perched on my shoulder, holding onto my dress as I ran. She stood watch, looking around for anyone that would do me harm.

As I sprinted past the stream, with the berry patch in sight, the slight pressure from where she stood lifted and I turned only to see her flying towards one of the creatures who had leapt across the river, its gaze intent on me.

It had *no* idea what Eira was, and how much power she wielded. I knew she would be OK as I continued on before glancing back to make sure she had the disgusting creature distracted.

An inhuman roar came from its mouth as she blasted it with magic, and I took that moment to slide quickly under the thorns and into the cool damp patch.

My breath came out with a *whoosh*, and I gulped in air and I calmed my breathing, only to startle when I realized there was another woman in here with me.

She had long silver hair and cerulean eyes that seemed to see into my very soul. Calmly she placed a finger to her lips. I had seen her before in the woods but couldn't remember her name. Leaning towards me, she took both my hands in hers, placing them on her temples.

Staring directly into my eyes, the blue in her irises swirled over and over and a voice spoke in my mind.

Don't be afraid. My name is Celeste, and I'm here to help. The Fomorians are here, and they will stop at nothing to kill your entire family, including you Becca. We cannot let that happen.

Her eyes beseeched me as she continued.

We will go to the old Oak and from there, I'll take you far away from all you have known. You must hide. Your bloodline is needed for the prophecy, and we cannot let anything happen to you or your future family. I want you to take my hand. We'll go quietly, and I will call upon my magic to keep you safe. You must believe me when I tell you that I will let nothing happen to you. Do you understand?

She let go of my hands and I stared, nodding shakily. The information she had just given me added to the stress of the situation, but she seemed steadfast in her belief that she could keep me safe, and now I had to be too. I didn't know what had become of my parents and siblings, or the rest of our family, but I could only believe it was nothing good.

Biting my lip, I followed her out of the brush and an energy like none I had felt before engulfed me. Tendrils of white smoke seeped from her fingers as she pointed her hands in different directions and her magic shot through the air, swooping through the branches of nearby trees.

The screaming lessoned, and pixies ran every which way around us, their eyes round with fear. Celeste grabbed my hand and we set off, quietly moving through the woods, keeping as far from the Fomorians as possible. Animals of every kind scattered. Mountain lions, deer, wild pigs, and the occasional fox leapt around us, all heading back in the direction of the village.

As our path took us beside the stream, naiads nodded at Celeste and swam towards the mayhem that was taking place. *"They will hold the Fomori off as long as possible to give us a fighting chance to get to the Oak."* Her voice whispered through my mind.

We burst into a clearing and the giant Oak loomed in front of us, auspicious in its nature. No one would ever assume that it was anything other than an incredibly old tree. With a whisper and a hand against the rough bark, Celeste took a look around before a door opened in the wood, a glow from inside greeting us as we stumbled in, and she quickly closed the door behind us.

The interior was enormous, and warmth radiated from a fire that crackled in the hearth. Looking upwards I saw there were many levels that reached as far as I could see. Books, and plants were interspersed with mystical items. I hadn't known about this place before, and I could understand why it was kept secret.

"We haven't time to look around now Becca, I'm sorry. We must get you as far away from the forest as possible, so they are unable to track you." Celeste's eyes flashed around the room frantically as if she were looking for something or someone. Concern shined bright in her eyes but was quickly banished as she shook herself and glanced back.

"Follow me."

Up the stairs we went, and upon reaching the fourth floor, she raced to a book, gesturing for me to join her. "Hold my hand tightly and don't let go."

Her eyes flashed white as she whispered a spell and the book that lay on the table in front of us burst open, expanding to three times its original size. The air around us became heavy and a swirling sensation began in my stomach.

Clenching my teeth, my body swayed and turned. Before I knew it, we were in a black void. Complete and total darkness. When my stomach finally stopped rolling, we were thrust into the brightness of day. A large lake loomed on one side, a field of tall grass graced the other.

"Celeste, where are we?" I asked, standing up and brushing off the dirt and leaves that clung to my clothes and hair.

"We're in Oklahoma. It's not incredibly far from home, but far enough away that I feel like you will be safe, and they won't be able to track you. Plus, I have connections here that will be able to help."

She turned, looking at me with sympathy shining in her eyes. "I know you've lost so much. We all have. But it is where you go from here that determines the rest of your life, and the lives of so many other Fae. Strength is something you have to hold tightly to, and you cannot let the humans around you know about our kind. They will never understand."

Greif and anger warred within me as I pictured what my parents and family must have gone through in their final hours.

I didn't know whether to weep or scream.

"Tell me everything Celeste. I need to know if we are to survive and as you say, fulfill the prophecy."

She told me everything and filled me in on the history of our people as we walked around the lake and towards a small town.

My parents always hushed my sister and I when we asked about the fae and witches' history. I always assumed that they were busy and just didn't have time to indulge our questions.

Now, I realized they tried to shield us from the wars and gruesome killings our kind had endured by the Fomorians. They feared what the Fomorians could potentially do to our worlds if they found the Keys that they so intensely searched for. It had to have been at the forefront of their minds. When I asked more about these mysterious Keys, Celeste said they were called; Dagda's Cauldron, the Spear of Lugh, The Stone of Fal, and the Sword of Light.

My mind whirled with all that our kind had been through; the wars they had suffered, the peace that they had found for a while, and now an old threat had reared its ugly head to try and take away all that we had gained.

And in some ways, they had succeeded.

I had no idea how many of my people had perished in our woods today, and my heart was heavy with grief and anxiety at what was to come.

Before long we reached the town, and Celeste took me to a cottage on the outskirts. Numbness consumed me as she opened the door, closing it gently behind us. Dust motes floated through the air in the rays of sun that filtered through the front windows. It was empty save a few pieces of crude furniture.

"I know it isn't much, but this is a safe house that I've had set up for a while. I hoped that we'd never need to use it." She walked to a doorway and opened it, gesturing inside. "The bedroom is here, and you'll find linens in the closet, along with towels. I'll come back soon with food for you to stock the kitchen, along with new clothing. You won't be able to wear those here." She waved her hand at my dress and I looked down at it forlorn.

Noticing my look, she raised an eyebrow. "Surely you understand that we need you to fit in as much as possible with the people here. A dress made from fairy weave will stand out like a sore thumb. It's imperative for you to look like the humans, and you cannot practice your magic anywhere it could be noticed. Do you understand?"

Not use magic?

My powers were so much a part of me, like a second arm, I never gave thought to using them daily. Here I was in a strange town, by myself and I would need to learn how to do everything without magic. Something ingrained in me since the moment I was born.

I thought back to my family, having died, all because an evil race was sure we would find the Keys and keep them from their terrible plot against the world. My mind was made up in that instant. I would do whatever I needed to make sure they didn't have their way. My family *would* live on to fulfill the prophecy. No mater what I had to do.

Later that evening while I dusted the old furniture off, there was a triple tap on the door. Celeste and I had agreed on that knock so that I would know it was her. Hurrying, I looked through the window beside it to confirm. Seeing her arms laden with packages, I quickly opened the door and let her in.

She swept into the house with the savory smell of fresh baked bread and spices surrounding her, and my mouth watered. I couldn't remember the last time I had eaten, but my stomach rumbled like it had been days.

"I wasn't sure what you would want, so I got a little bit of everything." She smiled as she began laying out the food on the kitchen counter. Meats, bread, cheese, pastries, and canned goods covered the expanse.

Once she was done, she put a kettle on the stove and made warm tea while I sliced the loaf of bread that had set my mouth to watering. We sat down to eat, and I had to keep myself from stuffing the whole piece in at once. Slowly I chewed, the sourdough flavor making my taste buds sing.

Curious to know what was next, I took a sip of my drink and looked at Celeste to find her watching me.

"You want to know what's next? Eh?"

"Yes. I'll do whatever is needed to make sure that the Fomorians don't take more from us. But I have no idea where to start. This place is different than anything I've known, and I feel lost." My insides quaked at the thought of venturing out into this new world alone, but I quickly tamped that down and grit my teeth.

"Becca don't worry. I'll look in on you from time to time, and make sure you're on the right path. This may be nothing like your home, or how you grew up, but the people here are not so different than you. The only difference is that they know nothing of magic, or the fae. They are just people who work hard daily to provide for their families. Inside they want the same things that we do, peace and a warm bed to go home to each night. Yes, there are some that do not have a kind heart, that may wish ill to other people, but the majority are not like that. You'll need to find a job, and work like the others. I'm sure that you will make friends, and before long you will settle into this life and be happy."

I had no idea what kind of job that I could get. Yes, I knew how to sew and how to cook, but other than that, I had no idea what I could make a living doing. No matter. I would just have to go into town tomorrow and see what was available. I would scrub floors if I had to.

Celeste smiled that knowing smile, and leaned forward, resting her hand on mine. "We're all counting on you Becca. Know that I have faith that you will do everything possible to help."

The color in her eyes swirled as I looked into them, pictures of events began flashing through my mind. There I was with a handsome man who had a devilish smile, a little girl running through a home holding a cookie and giggling, and then a young woman, holding another little girl who sweetly kissed her cheek. Next there was a flash of a different woman. Her eyes sparked evilness as she yelled to creatures that looked like the Fomorians, before blue fire eviscerated them. Fear struck cold in my heart as she stared at the young man and woman who stood before her. Her eyes turned cold with vengeance. There was also another man, a were shifter. So many pictures flashed through my mind of him and the same young woman, I couldn't get a handle on if he was good, or evil.

With a flash, the reel of visions stopped spinning in my head, and I looked back at Celeste as she let go of my hands. I didn't know what to think about all that I had seen, but deep down I knew that she had somehow given me a gift, a knowledge that would come in useful later on.

"Now, it is time for me to go." She stood up, and reached into a pocket of her dress, pulling out something that I could not see. "I want you to take this, and keep it hidden. Should you need me, place it in a bowl of water, and whisper my name." She handed me what looked like a pearl, small and round, its color changing as the light hit it.

I held tightly to the orb as she whisked out the front door, closing it gently behind her.

Chapter Two

• • • •

THE NEXT MORNING, I woke early, before the sun had risen over the trees. As I lay in this strange bed, I stared at the ceiling feeling forlorn. I missed my home, and all the things that had been comfortable. The covers that I used now were worn and scratchy. Nothing at all like the silkiness of the gossamer sheets that I was used to. The air didn't have the scent of flowers and herbs wafting through windows that needed no panes. And I wouldn't have my morning breakfast of fairy cakes that mother always made.

Tears stung the back of my eyelids and I bit the inside of my cheek hard to will them away. I didn't have time for them.

This was my life now. No spelled food, no fairy fabric, and no family.

Sighing, I rolled out of bed, determined to make the most of it and tried to imagine this as an adventure.

It took a while to figure out how to put on the new clothing that Celeste left for me, but once I finally did, I looked in the glass above the dresser. I had never worn trousers before. These were a rough blue and had pockets on either hip. The blouse was white linen, with round things on one side that fit through holes in the other. The shoes slipped on easy enough, plain and made from brown leather. I found these comfortable, but my feet were not used to having anything on them, and it was a strange feeling.

In the kitchen cabinets I found bread and tea. The contraptions to cook them, however, were daunting, and I gave up trying to figure them out, settling for cold bread and a glass of water.

Before long I was ready to set out and see what the town had to offer for a job. Outside the humid air clung to my skin and gray clouds filled the sky. I hoped it was not an omen for how my day would go. Ah well, it could be worse I supposed, as I set off down the dirt lane.

The town was not far from the cottage, and I reached it within a five-minute walk. There were people milling around, looking at the art and crafts that others sold from carts. A few glanced my way, curious I'm sure to see someone new. I smiled nervously and continued on until I reached a building that looked to be a grocer.

The door was strange, I could see right through it, and also my reflection in it. It must be similar to the looking glass that was in the cottage. The thought drifted from my mind as it opened and a young boy rushed out, followed by his harried mother, who glanced at me with a wary eye before rushing after the toddler.

I hurried in before the door closed shut and the sight of all different foods in bins, and more of those glass doors made me stop in my tracks. As did the counters where people stood, purchasing their items. The workers ran each one against some sort of machine and each time a noise would sound before the customers handed over their currency.

I had a lot to learn.

I strolled around the store for a bit, taking in everything that I saw. So engrossed that I startled at the voice behind me.

"Can I help you miss? I couldn't help but notice you weren't finding anything to your liking."

I turned around and an old man stood behind me, his glasses perched on the tip of his nose, a kindly look on his face. He had an apron on, and I imagined he worked here in some capacity.

Embarrassed, I looked around, my hands squeezing each other gently. "Well, I am new here, and I was just admiring all of your products. And also hoping to find someone to speak to about acquiring a job." The man looked at me closely, wiping sweat from his brow, then pushed his glasses back up his nose.

"Well Miss. I don't happen to have an opening here at the store right now, however my wife owns a flower shop down the way and needs a new employee. One of hers just quit last week, and she has been overwhelmed trying to do all of the work herself. I imagine she could use an extra hand if you're a hard worker and learn quick."

I was ecstatic at this news. While I would have taken any job available, working with flowers sounded like something I would enjoy.

"Oh yes! That sounds perfect and I will do my best for her and learn quickly. I do love flowers!"

He smiled and turned around. "Follow me, we'll ring her up really quick and I'll let her know you're on your way."

I followed him through the aisles to a room at the back. A small table and chair sat inside, the table littered with papers and a black instrument I'd not seen before. He picked up the top part of it and spun a wheel around a few times before putting it up to his ear. I was flabbergasted and watched intently as he began to speak into it.

"Hello dear! Yes, yes, everything is fine. I had a nice young lady come into the store looking for work, and suggested she come see you. She says she knows all about flowers and would be a hard worker." He glanced up at me with a wink. "Yes, I'll be sending her your way soon. OK, goodbye dear." Placing the object back down, he clapped his hands. "I have a feeling you two will get on nicely. Let's go outside and I'll point you in the right direction."

I wanted to ask this man, so badly what he spoke into, but I thought it would most likely seem strange to him that I didn't know what it was. I'd have to observe and figure out everything on my own from people around me.

"I'm sorry sir, it was silly of me not to have asked your name earlier. Mine is Becca." I looked his way as we walked out in front of his store.

"No worry at all. I am pleased to meet you Becca. I'm Jamie Taylor, and my wife's name is Lilly. You need anything at all, or if anyone gives you any trouble, you come tell me. We're a tight knit community, but every now and again there will be some troublemakers around."

Jamie pointed me in the direction of his wife's shop and waved to me as I headed off.

There were not a lot of shops lining the road, but I made sure to take notice of what all they were. There was a seamstress, a hardware store, a pharmacy, and right beside Lilly's Flower shop was a café. It was full of people eating and enjoying themselves, and I could see a woman smiling down at the couple by the window, refilling their drinks and placing food in front of them. I found it all very fascinating.

As I stared, the woman that was serving looked up and spied me through the glass. At first, she looked startled, but then smiled warmly and waved at me. Shyly I smiled and waved back before moving past the window to the front door of the flower shop. Pushing open the door, a bell tinkled above me.

"I'll be right with you!" The voice floated from the back of the store. In front of me flowers and plants of every kind graced tables blocking my view. The smell was heavenly and reminded me of home.

Around a big bunch of tulips, a small woman emerged. Her white hair was tied up in a bun, her mouth curved in a smile and eyes alight. "Well hello! You must be the young woman my Jamie called me about. Heaven knows I can use some help. This shop is busy on a regular day but around the holidays? It's downright chaotic."

"I can imagine! Well, I promise I am a quick learner and will work hard for you. My name is Becca by the way."

"Well Becca, I'm Lilly, and I am awfully glad to meet you. Come, I'll show you around the store and teach you how to use the cash register. We'll have you running this place in no time."

$$\infty$$

By the end of the day I learned what every flower in the shop was, though most of them were familiar. Lilly showed me how to use the strange contraption called the cash register and I had my first glimpse at money. Coins and paper that were used to buy things. So strange! In our village we bartered and traded. We did not buy things from each other, so it was a new concept for me. Observing her throughout the day, I learned that the object Jamie had spoken into was called a telephone, and you could speak to someone through it just by dialing their number.

Lilly went next door at lunchtime and returned with sandwiches and cold tea. The sandwich was divine, and something she called pickles gave a nice bite to it. I would have to have Celeste pick some up next time she stocked the pantry, or once I had money, buy some for myself. The tea was also different than any I had before. It was cold with ice in it, and so sweet that I felt as if I'd just ate a sweet cake. Lilly told me it was "sweet tea" but I didn't realize *how* sweet. Apparently, it was a drink everyone around here enjoyed immensely.

Once we had everything completed and ready for work tomorrow, Lilly turned out the lights and we walked outside where she locked the door.

"Becca, you have been a tremendous help today and I am amazed at how quickly you picked up on everything. I think we will be fast friends. I do believe that luck was on my side when you walked into Jamie's store today."

My heart burst with happiness that she was impressed with my work. I was incredibly lucky to have found the two of them.

Waving goodnight to her, I took off towards the cottage, the evening sky now cloud free, the sun setting behind the trees cast a multitude of pinks and blues. The birds sang and as I neared the cottage, fireflies danced around the trees and dragonflies swooped through the air. They at least, made it seem more like home.

OVER THE NEXT FEW MONTHS, I fell into a routine. Celeste visited me every so often, bringing food and other things she thought I might need. I enjoyed our visits and she kept me up to date about what was happening with the remainder of my clan. She explained how they found very few survivors and the ones that they did find had been taken to the Queen of Fairies castle to be cared for. Unfortunately, as I had feared, my family did not make it.

I mourned for them. I hadn't let myself give up hope until I knew for sure. I felt it in my blood though, that feeling of connectedness had disappeared shortly after the screams began that day.

There was nothing I could do about my loss now, except stay under the radar and make sure I did nothing to catch the eye of our enemies. So, I kept my days to only going to work and back, other than to stop in the grocery and chat with Jamie every so often. I made a few other friends through working at the flower shop, but no one that I let myself get close to. I spent most of my time at home, working on the flowerbeds and learning how to use the oven and stove.

Celeste showed me how to work the telephone, though who I would call, I had no idea. What I enjoyed the most, was when she asked for my help with potential spells to build the forest back up and spells to ward of the Fomori from entering it again. The hunger to use my powers was always satiated when I could let loose with someone and I didn't have to pretend to be someone I wasn't.

I finally got used to the strange clothing. The trousers were actually called jeans, and t-shirts were the soft tops that I often wore. She also brought some pretty dresses, but I had yet to wear them, until this morning.

When I woke to the sunlight streaming in through the windows, my soul just felt lighter. I had no idea why, but I decided to run with it. I was determined to be happy and more cheerful today.

I dressed carefully, braiding my hair, and putting on one of the dresses. It had red flower and floated around my shins. Twirling, I made the hem swirl out and it delighted me. Looking at myself in the mirror, I thought about the makeup women wore around town and I was curious. I didn't have any but surely a bit of magic wouldn't hurt if I did it inside the cottage.

Looking around, I instantly felt silly. No one could see me in here!

Laughing, I twirled my fingers through the air and my face was soon painted like the young woman in the grocery store. Not too much, just a bit of light color on my eyelids and on my lips. Pleased with my reflection, I left to go to work.

Humming as I walked, I was delighted by the children that played on the sidewalk. They giggled as they watched their friends play hopscotch and others threw a ball back and forth. I was surprised when one of them grabbed my hand and told me I had to play hopscotch if I wanted to pass by.

Amused, I smiled and told them I would. I studied the numbered blocks for a second and mimicked the best I could how the little girl before had done it. When I got to the end I turned around and she clapped, excited that I had played their game. Firmer clapping came from a man standing behind her who had obviously seen my silly display.

He had a smile that would stop anyone, with dimples on either side and a mischievous smile that made his eyes twinkle. A smile that I had seen before, and instantly I was stunned and speechless. My grin dropped as I realized I had seen him in the visions from Celeste.

I stood stock still as he walked towards me. That devilish smile making the corner of his eyes crinkle while they danced with laughter, presumably at my reaction to him.

"I apologize if I took you by surprise. I couldn't help but admire your hopscotch skills." He gestured towards the numbered blocks on the sidewalk. My cheeks heated and I looked down at my feet, not sure what to say to this man.

"Are you new here? I don't think I've seen you around before," he continued, and I looked back at him shyly and stammered.

"Ye... Yes. I just moved here a few months ago." I looked around, anywhere but into his dark eyes that seemed to see right into me.

"I see. Well, I'm not sure where you have been hiding, but never-the-less, my name is Derrick. And yours?"

I looked back to see his hand out in front of him, waiting for mine to shake it, his eyebrows hitched up in question. I knew I needed to fit in, so I quickly grasped his hand, and he gently pumped it up and down.

"My name is Becca. It's nice to meet you Derrick. But really, I must be on my way or I'll be late for work." I let go of his hand, instantly missing the feel of the rough, warmness of it.

He scratched the short stubble that graced his strong jawline and nodded. "Ah, well then Becca," he tipped an imaginary hat, "I'll see you around. Hopefully sooner rather than later." And with that he turned around and walked away.

∞

When the workday was over, my feet ached, but my heart felt happy. I found myself thinking about Derrick while the shop had a lull in business. The fact that I saw him in the visions even before we met, told me that he would somehow play a part in my life, though at this point, I didn't know if it was good or bad.

While Lilly locked the shop, I turned to her before heading home, emboldened since we had become close friends over the last few months.

"I met a man today on my way to work. I wonder if you know him?" She turned to study me as I continued. "He said his name was Derrick, but I've not seen him before."

Lilly's face broke into a wide smile. "Oh! That would be Derrick Hall, the town doctor. You might not have met him before because he usually is busy until late hours with his patients, and you my dear, don't socialize much." She chastised me, her eyes glittering with mischief. "So... tell me what you think?"

The look on my face was enough to cause her to chuckle, before linking her arm through mine. "Let's grab a cup of tea at the café and we'll have a chat. I think we deserve it after the busy day we had."

Inside the café buzzed with noise, just about every table was full, and Lilly led me to a booth near the back that had just been vacated by a couple. As we passed the counter, she raised her hand to the redheaded woman who stood behind it. I recognized her as the one that had waved to me through the window.

"We'll have one sweet tea, and..." Lilly looked at me.

"I'll have a cup of Earl Grey if you don't mind." I looked towards the waitress. She smiled softly and nodded her head. "You got it sweetie. I'll have those right out to you ladies."

"That's Regina. I went to school with her and she's one of my good friends. You ever need anything, you just let her know. She'll fix you right up. Soft heart that one has..." Lilly said as she slid into the booth, smoothing her hair back.

"So, you want to know more about Derrick then?" She questioned me. Again, I felt heat in my cheeks, but nodded quickly.

"Well, he was born and raised here. His father was the doctor before him, and when he retired, he was happy to hand the reigns over to his son. Derrick married his high school sweetheart, but it wasn't meant to be. They divorced after only being married two years, no kids, so it was an easy enough split. He's not been married since, but of course they only divorced three years ago. He's kept so busy he hasn't had time to date anyone new. But me? I think he's kept busy on purpose; he works himself too hard, doesn't give himself time for anything else."

She chattered on for a bit, but my thoughts wandered to Derrick and his mischievous smile. Before long we finished with our drinks and parted ways.

As I passed the grocery store, a tall woman with jet black hair leaned against the wall by the door. Her gaze was trained on me so intensely that the hair on my arms stood on end. Dark red lips pursed in distaste, and I glanced behind me to see if she could be looking at someone else, but there was no one. Increasing my speed, I looked away from her stare and passed by as quickly as I could, the feeling that I should know who she was so intense that I turned back to look again.

Only she wasn't there any longer, and I began to wonder if my imagination was playing tricks on me.

I quickly dismissed the strange woman and turned my thoughts back to Derrick, daydreaming about the handsome man who I hoped to get to know better.

When I turned the corner to the cottage, dragonflies flew around me, swirling and dipping through the air. I almost felt like I was back home, and that could only mean one thing.

Celeste was waiting for me.

Sure enough, she sat in the wicker chair on my porch, a smile wide on her mouth before she stood to greet me.

"Becca!" she exclaimed as she wrapped her arms around me. "From what I hear, you're doing splendid here... and what is that twinkle in your eye? That's new." She smiled as if she knew a secret. She already knew about my meeting Derrick; I could see it in her smile.

She was reading me again.

"Celeste, it's so good to see you. If you wanted to know how things were going here, all you have to do is ask. You don't have to read my thoughts every time, I'll willingly tell you all about it." I chastised her.

"Ah, but how fun would that be? You'd water it down, and I wouldn't get to see the full scope of how you're feeling. You forget, I know you and how you like to summarize. Plus, I have Regina to keep me up to date about what is going on around here." She laughed before following me inside.

"Well, only because I know you'll read me anyway. Why should I tell you everything when you already know it? And Regina? The redhead at the café is one of us?"

She nodded. "Yes, she is. She's been here for a long time, preparing in case we needed to use the safe house, and help out when we asked it of her. She will be there for you should you need her and will be on the lookout for anyone who might wish to harm you."

That made sense, and I should have realized from what Celeste said when she first brought me here about "contacts" in the town. Filing the knowledge away for later, I decided to get right to the point with her, there was no reason not to. "So, what do you know about Derrick Hall? I saw him in the visions."

She planted herself down in the kitchen chair, swirling her fingers through the air and produced two cups of her favored green tea, steam spiraling above them.

"Well..." she drawled. "You felt the pull to him earlier, yes?" I nodded the affirmative. "He is your destined one Becca. Though he is human and has no powers whatsoever, the universe knows he will keep you safe and love you with all that he is. He is imperative to your future, and your children's future. He will never know it, but that love and protection he will give you by affording a human life to you and your family will keep you safe, away from the Fomorians."

My head spun with the information. I wasn't sure how it all would work, but I had faith in what she said. I conjured pictures of a family with the handsome man that I'd met earlier and imagined the life we would lead. It was all very overwhelming.

"How will I keep my powers from him? What if I slip up and somehow, he finds out? He'd hate me forever!" I gasped as the thought bloomed bright in my mind.

She patted my hand and leaned forward. "I have a way to keep that from happening. You might not like it though. I can place a spell on you that will put a lock on your powers but will be reversable in case something goes wrong. Then you won't have to worry about causing any kind of suspicion. *And* it will keep the Fomorians from finding you should they wander this way."

I knew right then that I wanted her to place this spell on me.

It was the only way. Not having powers would also help me fit into this non-magical world. It wasn't so bad. I had made friends here that knew nothing of my past and magical ability, and they liked me anyway. The icing on the cake was knowing that Derrick and I were meant to be together. Though we had just met, the pull and the feeling I got while talking to him just felt *right* and lovely. My heart fluttered once more.

I looked up from the mug I was studying as I thought all of this. "I want the spell. Let's do it now." I said firmly, resolute in my decision.

She watched me quietly, and I knew she was doing it again. Once she was satisfied that I told her the truth and it was truly what I wanted, she stood up, reaching for my hand. "Well, let's get on with it, then shall we?"

Chapter Four

In the weeks after Celeste took my powers away, I felt lighter and free. Free from the fear of being found by the Fomorians, and free from the fear that I would inadvertently show them to the humans that surrounded me. I crossed paths with Derrick multiple times, and each time we got to know each other a little better, sometimes stopping into the café to have a cup of tea and talk. Regina always had a sparkle in her eyes when she served us. I'd yet to need her help though.

Other times Derrick and I simply strolled down the road enjoying each other's company. He was a lovely man. He made me laugh and was genuinely interested in all I had to say. There were times that I had to skirt around the truth. Especially when he wanted to know about my past and family.

I managed to put a believable spin on it, admitting my family had died and that I was alone in this world, trying to build a new life where I would be happy. He in turn opened up about his past marriage, and how the two of them had married too young with dreams of a perfect life, only to realize that their relationship was mostly built on the expectations from their families that they would be the perfect couple.

Derrick met me often after work, walking me home like the perfect gentleman, leaving only after he had seen that I made it safely inside. Lilly teased me ceaselessly about how she had never seen him act in such an old-fashioned way before with a woman, and I would always retort back that he just hadn't met the right one yet. She would always quickly agree.

Our relationship progressed in the months to follow and a year after weekly dates to the café or park, Derrick got down on one knee and professed his love for me. I had never been so happy, and had my powers been working, I would have thrown sparkles and fireworks into the sky to show my excitement. As I hugged his neck that day, black hair fluttered behind a tree, and I swear that the figure retreating through the woods by my home was the same woman I had seen the year before. All of my senses told me that there was danger. That *she* was the danger. But as Derrick swept me up in a passionate kiss, I was lost in his love, and the strange feeling disappeared.

We planned a small wedding with his family and our friends, and before I knew it, I was Mrs. Hall and the wife of a doctor. After moving into his house in the country and saying goodbye to the cottage that had seen me through that first year away from all that I knew, I felt at home. I still worked for Lilly and we enjoyed our weekly tea and chat sessions, but the time I spent with Derrick was immeasurable. He scaled back his practice and stopped working late into the evening. We would often dine together in the garden as the sun set on the horizon. There was nothing better.

At least that's what I thought, until I found out I was pregnant with our child, and I had the joy of knowing that we would have a baby together.

I was so immersed in the next nine months of planning for the baby's arrival, that I hadn't given much thought to anything else. Until the day Celeste dropped by the house while Derrick was at work, concern etched across her brows.

I hadn't seen her since the day before our marriage. She wanted to give me her congratulations and remind me of the orb that she left in my possession that I had hidden away, should I ever need her. We knew that she wouldn't be able to come around often in order to keep away any suspicion from Derrick. He knew nothing about Celeste, and we needed to keep it that way. We sustained our friendship through letters and phone calls.

Which was why I was at first scared by her presence, and also infuriated.

I ushered her in the house quickly, lest someone see her.

"What are you doing here?" I hissed quietly. I loved her, but I couldn't have her draw attention to herself, or me.

"I had to come Becca. You're about to give birth, and you haven't given one thought to the consequences it will bring. You should have called me sooner," she scolded with displeasure in her eyes. "I had to learn it from the fairies that Aine stationed around town to keep an eye on you."

My eyes widened at the thought that fairies had been hiding around town, and that I hadn't known it. I felt fear at what consequences she might mean.

"What do you mean consequences?" I demanded.

She sighed and sat down, squeezing her hands together in agitation that I had never seen her display before.

"Really? You haven't given any thought to your child having powers? Just because we put a spell on you doesn't mean that your fae powers won't be transferred to your daughter."

Surprise hit me in the gut at the revelation. I was having a *daughter*? Joy and fear at her words hit me at once.

I had not thought once about my baby being born with powers. Why hadn't I?

I suppose I had gotten too comfortable in my new life, surrounded by people with no knowledge about the magical world. Ashamed that I had been caught up in the romance of my marriage and our first baby, I looked at Celeste fearfully.

"What do I do?" I dropped down on the couch beside her, grabbing her hands. "Please Celeste. I am so sorry; I don't know what is wrong with me to have not even given that a thought. What can I do to make sure she is safe?" Fear coiled deep inside at the thought of the Fomorians finding her, and at the thought of her displaying powers in front of Derrick.

"Well, first of all. She won't come into her powers until around the age of sixteen. She is half fae obviously, but you do have a strong bloodline that will dilute her human side tremendously. We'll station more fairies around town and your home. They'll be invisible to the humans, so there is no worry about that. The fairies will put up a barrier around the town to keep any magic from being traced outside of it." She squeezed my hands. "It will all be ok. It has to be, for all our sakes."

When she left, images of the strange black-haired woman swam through my thoughts and I wished that I could call Celeste back and voice my concerns. I had a feeling that woman was nothing but trouble.

The next day I went into labor and our baby girl was born. Derrick and I were ecstatic. She was a beautiful little bundle of pink skin and dark brown hair. Gray eyes stared back at me from a chubby little face that I immediately loved more than life itself. I would do *anything* to keep her safe.

∞

We named her Selene, and she was the brightest star in our lives. Derrick was a doting father and husband, always making more time than he had for us, and eventually he hired another Doctor to help out with his practice so that he could spend more time with us.

Selene was an adventurous and fearless little girl. She ran through the gardens barefoot, playing with the wild rabbits that liked to nibble on the lettuce and cabbage that we grew, and dragonflies always found their way to her, dancing in the air and landing on her shoulders. They were drawn to magic, and I loved to see it, but it always caused a knot of unease to wind itself up in my stomach at what was to come.

Today was her tenth birthday, and she had asked not to have a party with her friends. When I asked why she smiled and held onto my hand tightly. "Because I want to spend it just with you and Daddy. Can we visit the lake again? I want to share some cake with the swans."

We went to the lake the weekend before, and to my surprise, two white swans had swum right up to us on the bank. Besides the fact that they were on a lake in Oklahoma was the fact that as Selene held out her hand to them by the waters edge, both had nuzzled her palm before turning around and swimming serenely off.

Later she told me that they spoke to her. I shrugged it off as a child's imagination, but deep inside, a part of me worried that her powers were manifesting earlier than expected. I had kept my eye out for any signs over the last week.

So, a visit to the lake complete with cake and milk was how we spent her birthday. Derrick and I lounged on a blanket while Selene played along the shore, kicking up sand and searching for unique rocks. She was disappointed when we hadn't spied the swans upon arrival, but we managed to take her mind off of it when we brought out her gifts. After squealing with glee at each one, and blowing out the candles on her cake, she took off in search of adventure.

Derrick and I laid on our backs pointing out the different clouds and what they looked like to each other when I heard her call for me.

"Mama! They're back!" I sat up quickly and saw that the swans were indeed back, and Selene stood thigh deep in the water while they swam in lazy circles around her. Her mouth moved as she prattled away to them, and my heart skipped a beat as Derrick laughed and asked if she was talking to them.

"Umm... She just loves animals of all kinds, you know that. She'd befriend a lion if she found one." I stated.

He chuckled and nodded in agreement before adding. "She has an imagination so big. And look at them, you'd think they understood her. It's the strangest thing to see a bird cuddle up to a person." The expression on his face was puzzled as he stared at the scene.

I scrambled to think of an excuse. "It looks to me as if they must be someone's pets. That's the only explanation for how comfortable they are with her. I bet they want treats." I feebly said.

Selene ran back up to the blanket where we sat, joy evident in her eyes. "They want some cake Mama. Can I have a small piece without frosting please?" Her eyes pleaded with me.

"Of course, sweetie." I scraped the white frosting off of a small piece before plopping it into her palm.

"Oh, they said that now did they?" Derrick laughed as he looked from his daughter to the graceful birds.

She smiled widely at him, her eyes lighting up. "Yep. They did!" And then she ran back to feed them their treat, and Derrick quietly watched after her while my stomach rolled.

Finally, he just smiled and shook his head. "She's going to write books one day. Mark my words. That imagination is something else."

My body slowly let the tension go as I realized that he had rationalized it in the way that I needed him to. I knew through the years it would only get more difficult.

Chapter Five

Selene

. . . .

IT WAS MY SIXTEENTH birthday and I was furious with my Mom for not letting me hang out with my friends. That's *all* I wanted. But no. She insisted that she needed me to stay home. That we would celebrate at our favorite lake with Dad, but she needed to talk to me about some things first. I rolled my eyes at her.

"Mom, I know about the birds and the bees. We don't need to have this talk today!"

Her gray eyes danced with mirth, and frustration sparked inside of me.

"Selene, I already figured out that you more than likely knew all about that. No, this is a much more important discussion that we must have. And now seems to be a better time than any since Dad is at work. Let's go out to the garden." Turning to walk away, she didn't even look back to see if I'd follow.

She knew I would. I would do anything for her.

We had been thick as thieves as I grew up, and no one knew me better. She indulged my imagination and didn't laugh when I told her about the swans, but she had asked me to not mention anything to dad. I never understood why, but I felt that it was important, and so I didn't.

I followed her to the herb garden that she and I lovingly planted years ago. I helped her pick out the dainty little bistro table and chairs that were surrounded by lavender and mint. The air around it was heavenly with the scents of all the herbs. Butterflies and bees flitted from flower to flower, soaking up all the pollen they could get.

This was a favorite spot of ours to talk. As I sat down, a small swarm of dragonflies floated around us, a few landing on my arms and head. It was nothing new, and I welcomed their presence. It just felt right and calmed me.

"So, what's up?" I took a swig of coke and leaned back in the chair, staring at her.

She cleared her throat and clearly looked uncomfortable. "I want you to keep an open mind as I tell you this Selene. It may seem outlandish and crazy, but it's all true. And before I start, I need you to promise me. Promise me that you won't utter a word of this to dad or anyone else. Not your friends. No one."

The hair on the back of my neck prickled at the seriousness in her eyes. "I promise."

She had my full attention now.

"You and I... well, we're not exactly as we seem. You've always been a little different, and I know you've noticed that. For example, your interaction with the swans. You spoke to them when you were little, you understood what they were saying. And the dragonflies," she gestured to the winged creatures, "they've always gravitated to you. There is a reason for that. You have magic inside you. So, do I, though I've been spelled so that my powers are dormant."

She was right. This was unbelievable. I began to wonder if she had hit her head, or maybe she was sick. "Are you ok? Should I call dad?" I interrupted her.

Violently she shook her head. "No! Do *not* call you dad. He mustn't ever know about this. Please just hear me out. I was born and raised in a magical forest not too far from here. One day horrible creatures entered and killed all of my family. I met a woman, a goddess really, who brought me here to keep me safe, and in turn keep you safe. You see, there is a prophecy that someone in our family will go in search of treasures, or

Keys if you will, that will save our world and possibly the human world as well. These creatures, the Fomorians or Fomori, want these items so very badly. To destroy all of the magical races so that they may be in power and rule. It's been this way for centuries. Celeste, the goddess who saved me, believes that we must be kept safe until the time is right for the Keys to be found. Once they are all recovered, they will be put together, forging a power that can be wielded to once and for all rid the world of the evil Fomori and all who work with them to destroy magic."

I sat in silence, stupefied by the information she just spouted. It seemed that she also needed a moment, as she took a deep drink from her tea.

"I know you still don't believe me darling. But we shall soon have a visitor that has promised to show you that all I say is true. Celeste should be here any moment. Please just remember that no one else can know about us. It would be extremely dangerous for them."

Right then a woman with long silver hair came around the side of the house. She wore a flowing dress and her arms and neck were draped with bracelets and necklaces. She looked like a beautiful gypsy.

Her eyes sparkled as she looked me over, her mouth curved in a smile.

"Ah, I may look like a gypsy, but of course by now, you know that I'm not."

Some of the dragonflies flew off to circle around her as she came to stand in front of me while I stared, dumbfounded.

"How... how did you know I thought that?" I breathed hard, my heart pounding.

"Everything your mom has told you is true, though I can help a little more if you would like? Can I hold your hands?" She gestured to them.

Without a word, I held them out and she squatted down in front of me so that we were eye level, gently taking them both in hers.

My vision blurred and her face fell away, scenes played out in front of me. Frightening and magical things, one by one until she gently let go, brushing the hair on my forehead back.

"Do you believe now?"

Gulping, I licked my lips that had suddenly become dry, and took another quick sip of my drink. I was overwhelmed and felt anxiety rushing in.

"Selene. Look at me." Celeste's voice was strong and clear, and extremely hard to resist.

I looked back at her serious face in front of mine. "What you've seen is all that our kind has been through, and why it is imperative that we find the Keys before the Fomori do. I do not think the one to do so will be you, although we had hoped that it would when your powers began to manifest early. Yes, your mom told me about the swans and any other little nuance that you produced. But you must know that it may come down to being one of your future offspring, and you must be ready and knowledgeable."

"Can you teach me?" I looked between her and my mom.

And so, it began.

I was immersed over the next few years in learning how to control my powers. They came and went sporadically, and it was hell to try and keep it all from my dad.

But he never found out.

I know there were times that he worried. I blew off all my old friends and spent more time with mom. A few weekends every year, we would tell him that I was going camping with friends, when really Celeste would take me back to Texas and teach me all the spells that I needed to know, and I met others from our race. It was overwhelming at first but seeing the visions that Celeste had given me steeled me for my first glimpses of fairies and all the new magic that surrounded me.

Mom had worried that the Fomori would somehow find me, but Celeste had assured her that the Queen of Fairy had scouts out everywhere while I visited and they would spirit me away as they had done her, whatever that meant, if and when someone threatened me.

The time flew quickly and all I could think about were the Keys. Graduation came and went, and I planned to take off a year from school with a promise to dad that I would go to college directly after that.

I planned to travel as much as I could and meet as many other magical beings that I could find. Celeste once again promised that she would and could protect me on my jaunt around the country.

She would travel with me.

While it wasn't exactly what I had in mind, I knew that she would be able to help me find these other people when by myself it might be difficult, since they didn't know me.

The summer was spent with my parents at the lake. Most of my days were full of sunning and nights were spent reading all I could on mythology.

On a particularly hot day I ended up going by myself to the lake. Dad wasn't feeling well, and mom had decided to stay behind in case he needed her.

"Don't be gone too long Selene and have fun!" She called as I ran to the car, ready to get away by myself. I loved my parents, but lately I felt smothered. Having to control my powers so much was wearing on me.

I rolled the windows down and put on some loud music before heading out. Just as I turned down the sandy lane to the beach, a lady walking by herself, her head turned down, caught my attention. When I slowed down, her head snapped up to look at me, black hair flying, and a ferocious snarl twisted her ruby lips. Evilness poured from her, startling me so much that I almost lost control of the car as I sped back up. All I could think about was getting as far away from her as possible. An unknown fear raced up my spine, and I glanced back in the rearview mirror, but she was no longer there.

I didn't stay long at the beach. Every time I tried to relax, fear caught up with me and I constantly surveyed my surroundings. By the time I returned home, I feigned a headache and went to bed early. I didn't want to worry my mom about my fears. Knowing her, she'd call in all of Fairy to search for the woman, and more than likely all that I felt was just a part of my overblown imagination.

After a few days went by and having not seen the woman again anywhere in town or on our recent excursions to the lake, I quickly forgot about her.

∞

At the end of summer, it was time to go. I stood on our porch, my mom hugging me hard, while I swear my dad fought back tears.

"Guys, it's only for a year. I promise to phone and write anytime I can. This will be good for me; I just know it."

Dad didn't know that I would have a travel companion, we thought it best, which would explain the mace that he stuffed into my purse as I turned to leave. I gave him another quick hug and raced to the taxi that would take me to meet Celeste.

Chapter Six

· · · ·

WE WERE FULLY INTO the fourth month of traveling, and I met all kinds of different creatures. Were shifters, more fairies, elves, and witches. Their covens were large and spread across the country, even the globe. I felt so free! Being able to use my powers when around them was a feeling like none other.

The majority of these groups were friendly and eager to meet me and show me how they lived their lives. I'd never been on a big vacation before, but this one was a journey of epic proportions. I learned so much in such a short time, and I thanked Celeste so continuously that she scolded me and told me not to mention it again.

I kept in touch with my parents, making sure to only mention the places I had been and adventures that were tame. The relief in their voices every time I called made me feel a little guilty as I knew they worried and wouldn't stop until I returned home.

In the fifth month we arrived in Colorado at a large compound high in the mountains. Snowflakes swirled around us as we hurried into the main home where we were to stay.

This place was owned by both witches and warlocks. They even had an Academy that Celeste felt I would be interested in. It welcomed all races. We were greeted by a large group that lounged around in the main room, and before I knew it, we were directed to our rooms with the promise of a day of adventure tomorrow.

It was late, so after saying goodnight to Celeste, I closed my door and wandered over to the long window. Pushing the curtains back, the view from this elevation was amazing.

Mountains surrounded us, rising high into the moonlit sky. Below the window a courtyard was illuminated by strings of lights wound through the trees and I made out two men sparring on the lawn. In the darkness they looked like two shadows twirling around in a graceful but dangerous dance.

As they did, their movements brought them into a beam of light from the moon, and one of them deftly knocked the other to his back. It seemed they were done. The one who stood over the other, reached out a hand and pulled him good naturedly back up, slapping him on the back, before glancing directly up at my window.

Never had I seen a more stunning man.

His dark hair shone in the light from the moon, and even from here I could see his piercing dark eyes. I knew he saw me highlighted from the light in the room, but I found I couldn't move. His gaze had me trapped in it, and it seemed he was under the same spell.

Slowly he smiled, his face brightening as he did. I waved slightly and smiled shyly, embarrassed that I had been caught ogling him. He gave a little salute to which his buddy saw and quickly glanced my way too.

The one that had caught my attention said something to his friend and they chuckled before glancing back up at me, then turning to walk back inside.

I let the curtain drop and felt a little lightheaded at the strange occurrence. I'd met many boys and men over the last few months, but none had sparked my interest as much as this one did. I knew I would most likely meet him tomorrow, and the thought made my heart skip a beat and anxiousness ran through my body.

I wouldn't sleep well tonight.

∞

Celeste had gone off to speak with some witches to plan a conference. Who knew witches and goddesses and all other manners of magical people held conferences? I didn't, until now.

I looked around the dining hall as I ate breakfast. Mine was pretty plain. Oatmeal and some fruit. I decided I didn't want anything too heavy to weigh me down through the day. Who knew what I might encounter or end up doing?

Around me, others ate a variety of meat and pastries. The other breakfast patrons milled around, exchanging pleasantries, a few smiling and saying hello to me as they passed by. I had purposely sat at a table for two, not wanting to strike up a conversation with a lot of people that I didn't know. At least yet.

Secretly I hoped to see the guy from last night with the beautiful eyes and smile, but he had yet to appear.

After throwing away the remainder of my breakfast, I wandered outside to the back lawn, marveling once again at the beauty around me. It couldn't be any more opposite than Oklahoma, and I was in love with it already. The yard was large, and as I walked, I realized that the edge of the lawn dropped off into a wide chasm. Standing there looking over it, I felt so small.

"Careful. I wouldn't get too close to the edge. You never know when erosion might make the ground weak."

The deep voice sounded behind me, and I took a step backwards before turning to see who the warning had come from. It was a good thing I did, because when I saw that smile beaming at me, I startled.

He was standing rather close and I marveled how I hadn't heard him approach. He was tall, much taller than I. As he looked down at me, I realized he was even more handsome than he had looked in the moonlight.

"Thanks for the warning. I guess I was just mesmerized by the beauty of it all. We don't have this in Oklahoma." I smiled.

"Ah yes, I've been there a few times. The mountains there are more like hills compared to these." He grinned. "So, you're the woman in the window. I hoped to run into you today. It took a little bit of investigation to find out who you were."

Embarrassed I looked down at my feet. "Yeah, sorry about that. I was admiring the view and just happened to see you and your friend. I promise I wasn't trying to stalk you."

He laughed loudly, and I looked back at him, the sound infectious. His teeth gleamed in the sun and he put his hand on my shoulder. "I never thought you were stalking me. But I plan on getting to know you a lot better. I hope you don't mind and end up thinking that I'm *stalking* you."

We spent pretty much the entire day together. His name was Rohn and he was a Warlock, a powerful one. He hadn't told me that but from the things his friend Cain said about him, I gathered that one day he would lead the clan. He was funny and outgoing, with a calmness about him that I soaked up like a sponge. I explained my travels, and also about the Keys. He was aware of them and the prophecy but not who or what was destined to find them.

Later I asked Celeste if we could stay here a little longer than we had planned. And of course, she had that look about her that told me she knew why. I didn't try to explain, but she took pleasure in asking me about Rohn every chance she got.

One day her words were more prophetic than usual and shook me to my core. We had been having some cookies and tea in one of the gardens when she suddenly leaned forward, her blue eyes swirling, and she quietly whispered to me.

"Mark my words Selene, he is your mate, destined for you, whether you know it now or not. He will be your beginning and end. The start of the prophecy is now, and he will share blood and magic to make it happen."

As she sat back again, her shoulders slumped, and her face was whiter than usual. "Are you ok?" I asked, concerned for the woman who quickly had become a close friend.

"Oh dear, I'm fine, those visions take a lot out of me though," she smiled quickly, but there was a darkness and uncertainty to her eyes that I had not seen before. "Go find your handsome man. I believe he's waiting for you."

Once I was certain that she was ok, I went in search of Rohn. I found him in a library reading, of all things. He was stretched out on one of the many couches, so engrossed in the book that he didn't even notice until I sat down at his feet. Scooting back in the plush cushions, I raised his feet and placed them on my lap as he looked over the book at me, a question in his eyes.

"Don't mind me. I'll sit here quietly while you finish reading. I just felt the need to be near you. So here I am."

A grin once again lit his face and warmed my heart. "There's no way I could concentrate on it now that you're here. Plus, I'd much rather your company than the books."

He swung his legs gently off my lap, and sat up, our hips touching each other as he put an arm around my shoulders, and I let my head fall against him. I felt his lips brush against my hair as he asked what was bothering me. I guess I hadn't quite learned how to school my features.

"Oh, nothing is wrong exactly. Celeste just had a vision, and I was basically told that you were my future." I laughed and looked at him to see a crooked smile grace his full lips.

Leaning even closer he brushed those lips against mine softly and whispered. "If she hadn't told you, I would have. We're meant to be together Selene."

And it was then that I totally and utterly fell in love with a Warlock.

We were married on that bright mountain, surrounded by the coven and magical fireworks flew high in the air. Our friends threw sparkles like confetti as we walked down the aisle as Mr. and Mrs.

Mom and I agreed that it wasn't feasible to have her and dad there with us since it would give away our secret. Instead we planned to have a small ceremony at home with them, and dad wouldn't be any the wiser that we had already wed. Though I hated deceiving him, I knew it was for the best.

We honeymooned in Scotland, and it was a dream come true. I had only thought that Colorado was beautiful, until I saw the Highlands and Lowlands there. Rohn showed me the fairy pools and made crowns for me out of the heather that grew along the road back to our hotel. And don't get me started about the castles. I certainly didn't want to go back home after our travels. But home we went, and when we arrived, I was swept into the life of the coven.

Though I wasn't a witch, Rohn taught me spells and also began my defensive training. He wanted me to be able to fight and defend myself should the need arise. By now he understood that there was a very good chance that I would be the one sent to find the Keys, or that our offspring would, and despite the romance that every day brought between us, there was real fear.

Rohn always tried to tamp it down with a phrase that I jokingly referred to as "Rohn's words."

Though we may not have all the answers now, one day we will. We will use our strength to make a better world, to bring magic and love to those around us when they need it most. We will be the light and bring sunshine to the darkness.

Even though I teased him about it, there was no denying when he said the phrase to me, whether whispered or with a bold triumph, that a calmness blanketed me, and all was right with the world.

What he didn't realize, was that he was *my* light.

Chapter Seven

• • • •

MORNING SICKNESS SEEMED to be the bane of my existence now. Every morning after a cup of warm tea, it hit, sending me running to the toilet to retch for ten minutes straight. Rohn tried every spell that he could think of to take it away, but nothing worked. I would just have to deal with it, and hope that it got better.

I was six months pregnant, and for six months I'd been dealing with it. When we visited my parents, dad told me that I should eat more, that I wasn't at a healthy weight. This I knew. But no matter what I did, nothing but my stomach grew. I wasn't losing weight, so at least that was a good thing.

When Celeste came to visit this morning, she took one look at me, and announced that the baby girl would have immense powers, and thus why I was so ill.

"Her power is trying to get out, even in the womb Selene. That is what is causing you to be sick." She looked at me with sympathy. "I can help, I think. But I'm going to need some extra power. Will you agree to let my friend Coeus come here? He's a Titan god, and with our powers combined we can at least make it more bearable."

She didn't have to ask me twice, I heartily agreed to it at the same time that I shouted for Rohn. He ran in so fast, that you'd have thought the house was on fire. A look of panic creased every line in his face.

"Sorry! Everything is fine. It's just that I have wonderful news. Celeste just confirmed that we're having a GIRL!" I jumped up and down

41

despite the baby weight. A look of joy replaced the concern as he swept me up in his arms and twirled me around.

God, I loved this man. He was my best friend and I could care less that he was about to be named head of the coven, a powerful and respected position. All I saw when I looked at him, was a man who was strong and sure, my rock and loved me deeply.

Celeste laughed as she watched us act silly and profess our excitement before waving and calling, "I'll be back with Coeus soon."

"Coeus?" Rohn asked, his eyebrow arched. "The Titan god?"

"Yes! That was another part of my news." I laughed. "She thinks between her and Coeus they can get rid of the morning sickness. She says that our baby is extremely powerful, and her powers are trying to work their way out of me, making me sick."

In my happiness about the baby and hopefully not being sick anymore, I hadn't thought about Celeste's words in much detail, but as Rohn's face fell, the information she had given me sank in.

He had caught on much quicker.

Our baby would live the prophecy. She would be the one expected to find the Keys and save all of us. If her power was as strong as Celeste said, we knew without a doubt it would be her.

Rohn reached out and pulled me tight to his chest, holding me as if he would never let go. We stayed that way for some time, quiet. Both of us lost in the tumult that our realization brought. Every fiber of my being fought against the realization that before she is even born, we knew that one day she will be in danger and at war.

Celeste and Coeus arrived, and together they worked extraordinary magic, causing sparkles to float through the air and a pressure built in the room. Rohn held tightly to my hand as they placed theirs on my stomach. Heat gently invaded for a short moment, and then receded when they were done.

Stepping back Coeus smiled, brushing his hands together. "You should feel much better from here on out Selene. And I must say, you've got one strong little lady growing inside of you. It's been such a pleasure to meet her and you. I imagine I will meet her again in the future. Try not to worry about her," he gave me a look of seriousness, "she will hold her own."

I believed him, but the worry wouldn't go away. For the next few months Rohn and I spent almost every waking moment together. We talked out our fears, read and gardened together. The rest of the coven knew that this time was ours alone and tried to give us a wide berth. Rohn must have ordered privacy, and I wasn't complaining.

When I was eight months pregnant, I went to my doctor appointment alone. Rohn had a meeting with the coven that he couldn't get out of, and I didn't mind. I could use some time by myself and thought I would stop into some of the stores while I was in town.

The doctor told me our baby was still perfectly healthy and strong, and happiness surrounded me as I stepped into a baby boutique nearby. It was probably a good thing that Rohn hadn't come with me, he would have died seeing all the girlie things that I had in my basket, and I'm sure the price tags wouldn't have helped. I chuckled to myself as I waited in line to checkout.

That was until I felt someone step up behind me, so close that I felt their breath ruffle the back of my hair.

"You can run, but you can't hide. None of your family can." A smooth sinister voice whispered in my ear.

Turning quickly, I backed into the person that had been in front of me, excusing myself at the same time as I dropped the basket. In front of me stood the same dark haired woman I had encountered all those years ago on the way to the lake. She had not aged a bit, and that sinister smile she once displayed was now full of anger and hate. I wanted to get as far away from her as I could, and without purchasing a thing I rushed out of the store, looking behind me as often as I could while managing to keep myself upright.

She didn't follow, but her words did. They echoed, over and over through my mind. Fear wound itself around my heart as I slid into my car.

I don't know how I got home. And I don't know how I managed to act so normal when Rohn came into our room later that evening. But I did. I couldn't let him know the danger we faced, or he would tear the world apart to rid us of it. This wasn't his fight.

It was mine.

∞

I took up knitting to rid myself of the overwhelming terror and to keep my mind busy and off the woman that I knew only meant my family harm.

After tearing out yarn multiple times, I finally got the hang of it. My first project was a dark blue knitted beanie. I had this idea, where it came from, I had no idea. But I wanted the hat to be spelled with a specific kind of magic. The thought came to me as I held the soft hat in my hand, and I called to Rohn.

"Honey, can you do me a favor?" And he grinned and grinned. Probably because he had been hearing that question daily now. But he never once complained. After I explained what I wanted, he was happy to help. He said it was a rather easy spell and I watched in fascination as he used a coat as an example to show me how to do it.

I gave him other specific instructions about how I wanted the spell and I knew that it was asking a lot, but I felt it was imperative for the future. I just knew that it would be of some help when it was time for the journey to find the four Keys.

He stared at me, but finally gave in and taught me the words. "Ok Selene, do exactly as I showed you."

I held it in front of me, whispering the words and swirled my hand over it first clockwise, then counterclockwise, before blowing my power softly onto it.

"That should do it." He held his hand out to help me up so that we could retire to bed for the night. Before I followed him, I gently tucked the hat into a chest at the foot of our bed. It wasn't for me; it was for our daughter.

$$\infty$$

• • • •

ANDIE WAS BORN TWO years ago on a night when the moon streamed in and dragonflies flew through the open window to alight on my bed. When her first cries were heard, the coven rejoiced and had an epic party for days in her honor.

Now as I gazed at her bent over her doll, playing, my heart squeezed with love. Never in our wildest dreams had Rohn or I imagined that we could love another the way that we love her. She is our sun, moon, and stars. Everyone that met her was drawn to her quiet and calm personality. She has strength even at two years old, a strength rarely seen. Even now, she knows what she wants with an uncanny maturity.

She began talking at sixteen months old, and from that moment on she would tell us what she wanted, and most definitely let us know what she *didn't* want. The dragonflies delighted her, drawn to her as they had been to me, and she would speak to them as though they held a conversation all their own.

There were times I caught her alone in her room, sparkles filling the air, and toys floating to join them. I felt real fear whenever I saw her manifesting her powers.

It was *too* early!

Though we tried to make life normal for the three of us, Rohn and I stayed fearful. The thought of something happening to our precious girl was too much to think on.

And so, began my search for the Keys. Despite Rohn's protests, despite my mom's cries and Celeste's warnings, I knew I had to do something. And I would not let my daughter be caught up in a war that she didn't ask for.

Not if I could help it.

Did you enjoy The Four Keys? Please help recommend it to others by leaving a review. They really do make a difference!
Thank you!

ALSO AVAILABLE BY J.C. LUCAS
Sword of Light (#1 The Four Keys series)
https://www.amazon.com/gp/product/B088DKTL4C
COMING SOON:
Cauldron of Hope & Sorrows (#2 The Four Keys series)

....

IF YOU'D LIKE TO BE one of the first to know about new releases or sales, click below to sign up for J.C.'s newsletter. Just subscribe to her website and you'll get all the news!
https://www.lucasjc.com/
Let's be friends! I'd love to connect with you!
Instagram: @j.c.lucas_author
Twitter: @lucas_author
Facebook: https://www.facebook.com/j.c.lucas.author
Goodreads: https://www.goodreads.com/author/show/20415558.J_C_Lucas
Bookbub: https://www.bookbub.com/profile/j-c-lucas-7fadf941-1617-4680-b878-53409fa91e17
Pinterest: https://www.pinterest.com/jclucas20/
If you're interested in being on my ARC team or have any questions or just want to give me a shout, email me!
jclucas78@lucasjc.com

For a sneak peak at the first two chapters of Sword of Light, the first book in The Four Keys series, turn the page.

Sword of Light
The Four Keys, Volume 1
J.C. Lucas

· · · ·

Published by J.C. Lucas, 2020

Chapter One

At sixteen, I didn't expect to have to deal with another death in the family. Even in my wildest dreams, I never imagined I would be sitting in a social worker's office, waiting to be taken to a new home. Yet here I was, a week after my nan died, with no family, no close friends, and no idea what my future holds.

Fiddling with the strap on my bag, I looked around the mundane office wondering where the social worker had gone off to this time.

Anne had swooped in the same day that the ambulance took Nan to the hospital. She had picked me up from school and rushed me to Nan's side, just as she took her final breath. I held onto her cold hand for hours, numbness taking over before Anne finally pried me away.

She pulled me from the hospital room, murmuring nonsensical words to me, but I hadn't paid any attention. I stared back at Nan as we walked away, my heart a heavy lump in my chest, my eyes burning from the tears that I had shed.

It was at that moment, as Anne shuffled me away from the woman who had raised me, that I noticed soft lights swirling around her body, faster and faster through the air until they disappeared. At the moment, I had chalked it up to distress, exhaustion, and maybe the headache that had been pounding behind my eyes. But as I sat here now, thinking back on that day, I was sure that I hadn't imagined them.

Anne strolled around the corner, a tall man following behind her. He wore a suit and tie and carried a fancy briefcase. His stature next to Anne's shorter one made her appear as if she were only four feet tall. The guy, who looked a little like the used car salesman who always ran cheesy ads on TV, raised his eyebrows as he looked me over before dismissing me to once again chat with her.

I really didn't care who he was, but his response irritated me for reasons I didn't understand. Fear about what would happen rippled through my body. Would the slimy-looking man take me somewhere I didn't want to go? My breath came quicker as anxiety began to set in. It seemed to happen a lot lately. It made me lightheaded, my chest tight, and caused me to feel as if I were spiraling out of control.

Gritting my teeth, I resolved to be tough and tamped down the cold feeling, putting it away in its own little box. I would get through whatever was next by myself. I didn't need anyone.

Curling up in the backseat as close to the car door as possible, I couldn't help but stare at Anne as she talked to herself. She kept looking over at her purse, giggling and shaking her head. *She's so weird....* A few days ago, I decided that she must have a screw loose or some kind of chemical imbalance.

Her laughter made my ears burn now, and rage festered inside me. How could she be happy when my world had been torn apart? She could at least try to act like she cared that Nan died. Why couldn't she put herself in my place and see how horrible it felt for me to leave my home? Here I was, going to live with someone I had never met before, and she was laughing! I couldn't believe how insensitive she was.

Narrowing my eyes, I stared daggers at the back of her head.

The rain picked up as we sped down the highway to Junction, and outside the window, tall trees obscured everything else. They were so different from the trees back home. Not at all like the red cedar or spindly pecan trees that dotted the landscape in North Texas. These trees soared high into the sky, growing so thick together that it was impossible to see through them. Huge oaks and towering pines grew together in masses. What would it be like to climb to the top of one and sit so high above the rest of the world? I imagined myself up there, screaming my anger at the world. It might at least make me feel better for a little while.

"Andie, are you doing okay back there?"

I glanced at Anne and caught her looking at me in the rearview mirror with wide green eyes. Remaining silent, I gave her a blank stare as she looked back at me, her eyes scanning mine in the mirror. I was furious that she even dared to talk to me. She should be used to this by now. Not once had I responded to her since she picked me up, and I wasn't about to this time. Who did she think she was? She didn't care, not for one minute.

Huffing, I turned away from her to gaze out the rain-streaked window again. She probably thought I was a brat. And honestly? I didn't care.

Anne turned the car onto a dirt road lined with more trees, and we bumped down the rock drive. At the end, tucked away with tall trees appeared a small white house. Flowers of every color decorated the landscape, brightening the dreary day. As the car pulled up in front of the house, there were no other homes visible from where I sat. The surrounding woods encased the home, and trees were all I could see for miles.

This place was so different than what I was used to. Nan's house had been in a suburb, with cookie-cutter homes. Each one had been the same, side-by-side with no yard to speak of. I was never fond of the proximity between them and rarely opened the curtains in my bedroom for fear that the next-door neighbor might look in. I wouldn't have to worry about any neighbors here, that was for sure.

"Andie, I know you don't want to be here, but Celeste was your Nan's friend and she agreed to take you in. This place will grow on you, I promise. There's so much waiting for you here."

Again, she peered at me in the rearview mirror, and I shrugged, looking away from her while she lumbered out of the car. She was short and broad but carried herself as if she were a six-foot-tall duchess. Her long brown ponytail swayed in time with her hips.

I sat in the backseat with my arms crossed, watching her before looking over what was to be my new home.

The screen door at the top of the porch opened and an older woman wearing a long blue skirt and a flowing white shirt stepped outside. Her gray hair was long and braided, her face remarkably unlined for someone her age. *Must be good genes*, I thought, curious about the lady I would live with. She glanced at me, smirking as if she was aware of some inside joke that I wasn't privy to.

Walking over to Anne, she wrapped her in a hug.

I wonder how they knew each other. The familiarity between the two made it seem as if they were friends. They spoke for a moment before the woman patted Anne on the shoulder and headed over to the car. Opening the back door, she leaned down to look at me with eyes that were a bright sapphire blue and seemed to see into my very soul.

"Hi, Andie. It's so good to finally meet you. I'm Celeste. Won't you come inside so we can visit for a bit and get better acquainted? I've been awaiting your arrival all day."

She smiled warmly and seemed genuinely happy that I was there. It seemed strange that someone would willingly open their home to a sixteen-year-old teenager who they'd never met before. For all she knew, I could be a serial killer or a thief who would rob her blind.

She reached inside the car, her face relaxed and her eyes sparkling. I did not doubt that Anne had told her all about my crummy attitude, so it surprised me that she seemed so accepting. Glancing down at her hand, I hesitantly grasped it with my own. Warmth raced up my arm, and a tingling peacefulness took over, easing the tension in my body. Baffled by it, I pondered where it came from.

I unfolded myself from the backseat, stepping out of the car. Anne already had my bags in both hands and my backpack slung over her broad shoulders as she shuffled to the steps.

Celeste continued to hold my hand as she led us up to the porch, the strange warmth racing from her hand to mine. I was floating in the cozy feeling as we walked up, and I felt too tired to question it.

Looking around the porch, I spotted a sign by the door that stated, "Haven." Those words hit me hard in the gut, tugging at emotions I had kept bottled up for the last few days. Heck, the last week since Nan passed. She had always been my *Haven*. My safe place, the one I always thought would be there for me. Losing Nan was the hardest thing I had ever been through in my life.

I never wanted to feel like that again.

I couldn't remember either of my parents. Mom died when I was two, and my father disappeared soon after. No one knew what had become of him. Not a single letter was sent. Not a payment made on any of his credit cards. Everyone just assumed he was dead.

Nan had been the one constant in my life, and like any teenager, I had taken for granted she would be around forever. My chest ached and tears pooled in my eyes, so fresh was the pain from her loss. I turned my head away from Anne and Celeste to hide my despair. I couldn't bear for anyone to witness my pain.

As if sensing what I tried to hide, Celeste squeezed my hand a few times before gently letting it go to usher us into the living room. It was bright, with a ton of plants scattered around. The greenery gave the room a clean and peaceful vibe. A sofa sat in the middle of the room, looking worn but comfortable with blankets draped over the back, and knickknacks littered various side tables. What caught my eye, though, was a bookcase covering an entire wall, floor-to-ceiling, with every shelf full of books.

Celeste and Anne talked, but their voices became only background noise as I wandered over to the gorgeous bookcase, running my fingers over the spines of classics and old books I had never seen before. It was amazing! My love of books and my despair at having to leave all my favorites behind was completely and utterly washed away by seeing this wonderful display.

Nan always said I had an old soul. She indulged my love of books and would take me on a weekly trip to the local bookstore to let me pick out one book each time. I was always cautious, taking my time to make sure the book I picked out was one I would read and enjoy multiple times. It had to fuel my imagination and draw me in so much that I got lost in the story, imagining I was part of the adventure. For the most part, every book I got did just that. I'm sure some people would say I'm a nerd, but I wouldn't care. A lot of the time, I found that reading books was better than being around most people.

Looking at all the different titles, I noted which books I wanted to read while I was here. The books were a bright spot in this situation. But Celeste and Anne didn't need to know that. I hoped if I were enough of a brat, they'd return me to my old home, as silly as that hope might be.

Scowling, I turned around and plopped down in the most unladylike manner possible, causing Celeste to raise her eyebrows. She studied me but surprisingly made no mention of my rudeness.

Walking over, she and Anne sat down, both watching me, perhaps waiting for an outburst. I rolled my eyes, staring at the books in front of me. I would not give them the satisfaction.

Celeste cleared her throat, breaking the silence. "Becca—well, your nan, was an extraordinary friend. We met when we were young girls. You remind me so much of her. It's uncanny! Even though I hadn't seen her in years, we wrote to each other as much as possible. So many of her letters were about you and how much joy you brought her. One day, I'll let you read them if you like. You were her entire world. I understand that you're having a tough time, but I hope you'll let me help you get through this."

My stomach clenched as I pushed down the feelings her kind words evoked in me. My emotions were all over the board, and I didn't want to be that weepy girl everyone pitied.

Toying with the fringe from the blanket hanging over the back of the couch, I tried my hardest to act indifferent. I didn't want Celeste to know I was hanging on to her every word.

The women shared a knowing look and rose to walk together toward the front door. They murmured to each other for a while, but no matter how hard I strained, I couldn't make out what they were saying. Anne turned back, talking to herself again, and looked around the room.

What was she up to now?

Spying a book lying on an end table, she exclaimed, "AHH, there you are! Don't be stealing my thunder again!"

She gave the book a crazy evil eye, and I tried to figure out what the heck she was going on about. Gazing back at me, she smiled, wiggled her eyebrows, then snorted before turning away to walk outside with Celeste, leaving me bewildered.

Staring at the book, I tried to make sense of what I had witnessed. The book was thick and covered in brown leather, the title not visible as the backside of the book was face up. Looked like a normal book to me, albeit an old one.

Shaking my head, I stood up from the couch, stretching my arms above my head to relieve the tension in my shoulders. A strange noise came from the next room, and I lowered my arms to listen.

What was that?

The sound drifted through the air again, and I realized it was someone whistling. Curious, I followed the sound into a sunroom filled with different plants and flowers. Some were regular houseplants, and others were tropical. The sweetness of jasmine permeated the room, tickling my nose. The whistling grew much louder as I walked around a pair of tall bamboo plants.

And there it was. A birdcage with a beautiful blue parrot swinging on a perch, whistling its heart out. The parrot's eyes were closed as it whistled, while it swung back and forth on the little wooden swing. It seemed content, and happiness rippled off its feathers. A giggle rose in my throat before bubbling out at the funny picture the bird made. I slapped my hand over my mouth to muffle the sound.

I shouldn't be happy—definitely not giggling! I frowned at the parrot for making me laugh, as if it had done it on purpose. Opening its eyes, the bird cocked its head and squawked at me.

"Hello!"

Its eyes were wide and staring at me as if it were waiting for me to say something back. Staying silent, I watched it tilt its little head side to side and step from foot to foot.

"Hellooo!"

The volume of the screech startled me, and I jumped high in the air, putting a hand to my chest as my heart beat erratically. Jeez! This bird has some lungs!

"I see you've met Charlie." Celeste glided into the room, smiling fondly at the parrot. "He found his way here with a hurt wing, and I did my best to heal him. We've been friends ever since, and let me tell you, he keeps me on my toes. Charlie is quite the chatterbox, and it's always a mystery what he will say next." Walking over to the cage, she leaned in as Charlie leaned forward, and she kissed the tip of his beak.

"Love you, love you!" The bird sang to her, preening from side to side. He turned his head to look at me as if expecting me to kiss him too. *Nope. Not going to happen.* His skills were impressive and all, but kissing a bird is not my thing. Shaking my head, I gave him a disgusted look before walking over to the large windows to gaze at the surrounding woods. Chatty Charlie prattled on in the background as I looked out.

I had never seen so many tall trees in one place. The woods were thick, and the darkness called out to me, promising solitude, and an escape from reality. I couldn't wait to explore. It was strange, but there seemed to be a pull on my soul to go there now.

Celeste called to me and I shook the strange feeling off. She must have said my name a few times, trying to get my attention.

"Dear, are you all right? You were lost in your thoughts. Why don't we go upstairs, and I'll show you your room? Then we can have some tea and chat awhile. Or if you prefer, you can rest a bit. Whatever you'd like." She gestured to me, and I quietly followed her through the house to the stairs.

Halfway up, art hanging along the wall caught my eyes, and I stopped to study one of the paintings. It was a picture of the night sky filled with stars painted so beautifully that it was as if they really twinkled. Underneath the diamond-laden sky lay a green forest with small golden lights sprinkled throughout the trees. Fairies peeked out between leaves, as others danced around a circle of stones on the ground below. Each one wore delicate dresses made of flowers, and tiny slippers made of leaves. Inside the circle of stones sat a book with a glowing symbol gracing the cover. The ethereal quality of the painting was stunning. Whoever had painted it was exceptionally talented.

We continued up the stairs. The bedroom Celeste brought me to was gorgeous, and I mumbled as much as I walked around. A small white desk sat under a large picture window, with writing instruments and paper laid out. I imagined myself sitting there on a beautiful day, writing, doing homework, and looking out the window. At night, I would watch the moon shine down on the top of the great oaks. A full-size wrought iron bed rested against the wall, the coverlet, white with tiny blackbirds, and pillows were piled high. I longed to jump on the softness of them and wallow around.

Celeste also showed me the adjoining bathroom, which was small, but a good size for me. Toiletries, makeup, and a new toothbrush sat by the sink. She had thought of everything I might need. Even though I wanted to go home, this place didn't seem too bad.

"I'll leave you here to unpack your things and get comfortable with your new room. If there's anything you think of that you need, please tell me. We can run to town anytime you like, and tomorrow we head that way to get you enrolled in school. Come on down when you're ready, and I'll fix us a nice cup of hot tea." Celeste smiled before shutting the door behind her.

Ugh, school.

I didn't even want to think about going to a new school. It gave me anxiety, worrying about how everyone would treat me, the new girl. I had friends back at Central High, but no one I had been really close to. So many of the kids at my old school were entitled brats. Their parents bought them anything they could ever want, not what they needed. They were only friends with other kids just like them, who were obsessed with themselves and changed friends on a whim. I had always tried to steer clear of them. Who wanted friends like that?

Definitely not me.

After putting my meager belongings away, the closet still looked empty. My wardrobe only comprised of jeans, old T-shirts, cardigans, and my favorite Converse tennis shoes. I didn't care about clothes and what was "in style." I liked being comfortable and having my own look; Nan had always encouraged me to be myself. So that's what I did. She used to tell me how "cute" I looked in my beanie and glasses. I had yet to find any reason to try contacts. The thought of sticking something in my eyes grossed me out, and I wasn't ready to submit myself to that torture.

My beanie was the one thing I would never give up. It was a tried-and-true staple of my wardrobe, no matter what the weather was, and no matter what I was wearing. I found it in Nan's hope chest when I was nine. When she told me, it had been my mom's, my nine-year-old self had clung to that beanie and wore it every day. It was my security blanket from that moment on. It's silly, but somehow, I felt by wearing it, it somehow made me closer to the woman I had never known.

Making my way downstairs, I followed the smell of cookies until I found myself in the kitchen. Celeste sat at a table, sipping a mug of tea, and reading the same book that crazy Anne had been talking to. I eyed it warily, half-expecting some monster or genie to jump out. When she heard me enter, Celeste closed the book and set it aside, face down.

"Would you like some green tea, Andie? I've got some in the teapot."

Nodding, I sat down on a barstool by the kitchen island, swinging my feet as I looked around the room. It was clean and comfortable, with herbs lined up in pots on a shelf, and cookies cooling on a rack, their aroma floating through the air. Taking a deep breath, I savored it. That delicious aroma was familiar, and memories of making the cookies with Nan made my heart twinge.

"Here's your tea. I made snickerdoodles. I think I remember your Nan telling me she always made them for you. I hope they're as good as hers."

No one baked snickerdoodles as good as Nan.

A lump of sorrow welled up in my throat, and I swallowed hard to force it down. It didn't work very well, so I sipped the hot tea and stuffed a cookie in my mouth. Hopefully, she didn't notice the emotion on my face; Nan also said I would never make a good poker player.

I chewed the cookie, marveling at how they tasted so much like the ones I grew up eating. I wondered if Nan had shared her recipe with Celeste. Swiveling my chair around to face her as she took a seat at the table, she was studying me, not critically, but with patience and understanding. She was waiting for me to speak up; I could tell from the look in her eyes. So, I did.

"Celeste, how did you and Nan meet? I don't remember her ever talking about you, which seems kinda strange if you were such good friends. Maybe I wasn't paying attention, but since I'm supposed to live here with you, I think it's fair to ask."

She smiled and began her story.

"Your nan and I met when we were both around your age. She had a vibrant soul, full of energy and curiosity. Somehow, she got lost in these very woods one evening. I was out there too and came upon her as she was trying to find her way home. Oh, she looked a right mess with grass in her brown hair, her knees dirty from stumbling a time or two. She was so grateful, and she held onto me the entire time I was leading her home. From that moment on, we were fast friends. We fought a lot of life's battles together in our younger years, and we were inseparable until she met your grandfather. That's when we drifted apart. We wrote to each other for years, sharing heartaches and happiness. I also visited her once when your grandfather passed away. It was a nice visit, but she was distraught and had a lot going on so I didn't stay long. There were a lot of important things she had to take care of, and I understood..." Celeste drifted off, a faraway look in her eyes as if lost in thoughts of the past.

She had a way of making things sound so mysterious, which only made me want to press for more information. I wanted to know more about Nan and her life that I was never privy to before, but Celeste had closed the conversation. I would just have to wait.

We discussed the school I would be going to, and Celeste went on and on about it. She thought it was a great school. Time would tell. We were going there tomorrow, and she would sign me up to be a student. My stomach clenched at the thought. She also mentioned we would stop at the store to pick up whatever supplies I might need, and she wanted to take me to lunch at a café one of her friends owned. She raved about the food and how much she thought I would enjoy it.

With all the talk about what we would do, I warmed a little to the idea and looked forward to a normal day. Once the sun set, we had a small dinner consisting of salad and warm bread. It was simple but good, and I relaxed more than I had in a while, enjoying her quiet companionship. I was grateful she didn't push me into talking about how I was coping with everything. Right now, I just couldn't talk about it without getting emotional, or angry.

Not long after, I headed up to bed, hoping to sleep without the regular nightmares appearing. As I lay down on the pillowy softness of my new bed, sleep dragged me under.

Running through the dark woods, fear overtook me. Heavy footfalls caught up and had my stomach clenching in horror. I pushed my legs to go faster, and my breath crystallized in the air as I panted from exertion. Frantic, I couldn't stop. I knew it would kill me. I dodged through trees that displayed four-point stars with twisted knots inside of them glowing on their rough bark. The sight of those stars burned into my brain, and somehow, I knew they were important.

Moist breath whispered over the back of my neck, reminding me I didn't have time to worry about the symbols. Whatever was chasing me had caught up, and the terror I felt was overwhelming. Tumbling, I fell to my knees, rolling over to jump up to face my pursuer. My eyes widened, and my mouth fell open in horror as I stared at a giant man standing menacingly in front of me. Pale white skin stood stark in contrast to the midnight black of his armor. He sneered down at me, and jagged teeth filled his mouth as saliva dripped from the corners. Lifting a razor-sharp spear high in the air, a hideous noise sounded low in his throat, and soulless black eyes pierced me. My body moved as if it already knew what to do. Like a puppet on a string, I jumped with feet raised, kicking my legs hard into his chest. The hit catapulted him through the dark woods, his body disappearing into the forest while all the glowing symbols on the trees dimmed and faded.

Want to read more? Click below to continue Andie's epic journey full of magic and mayhem!

Sword of Light (The Four Keys series, Book 1)

https://www.amazon.com/gp/product/B088DKTL4C

COMING SOON: Cauldron of Hope & Sorrows (The Four Keys, Book Two) – October 2020

ABOUT THE AUTHOR

. . . .

J.C. Lucas lives in Texas with her husband and three sons. She grew up writing fantasy stories and dreaming of the day when she could share those stories with the world. J.C. is an avid reader of many genres, loves to garden, and cuddle with her mini dachshunds. Coffee, wine, and dark chocolate are some of her favorite things.

For more information about the author, check out her website at:

https://www.lucasjc.com/

Let's be friends! I'd love to connect with you!

Instagram: @j.c.lucas_author

Twitter: @lucas_author

Facebook: https://www.facebook.com/j.c.lucas.author

Goodreads: https://www.goodreads.com/author/show/20415558.J_C_Lucas

Bookbub: https://www.bookbub.com/profile/j-c-lucas-7fadf941-1617-4680-b878-53409fa91e17

Pinterest: https://www.pinterest.com/jclucas20/

If you're interested in being on my ARC team or have any questions or just want to give me a shout, email me!

Jclucas78@lucasjc.com

Acknowledgements

Thank you so much to my new readers for reading the Prequel to the Four Keys series. I hope you enjoyed learning about Becca and Selene. And thank you to all my readers who read Sword of Light and have left such wonderful reviews. Thank you to all my friends and family who have encouraged and supported me. It means the world! Thank you to my Mom for her endless enthusiasm, beta reading and cheering me on. Thank you to my husband and children for always being patient while I'm in writing mode and making sure I eat. Thank you to my awesome cover artist, Maria Spada. She brings my ideas to life in a way that only she can.

. . . .